CW00866693

ISBN 0-86163-778-X

First published 1995 by Award Publications Limited,
27 Longford Street,
London NW1 3DZ

Printed in Singapore

Tales of Monsters & Beasties

Illustrated by
JANE LAUNCHBURY

AWARD PUBLICATIONS LIMITED

Contents

Daring Daisy and the Dragon

by Maria Gordon

It was Daisy's birthday and this made her sad. It just didn't seem right to open presents in the dark, whisper instead of sing "Happy Birthday", and never, ever play any games. She tried to be pleased that she was the only village child to have her party at the castle. But she really didn't think that the dungeon was the right place. Daisy did her best, but this year no one could cheer her up. She said her thank-yous politely and helped clear up before the rats sneaked in. Then she took herself off to the corner spyhole, the only spot with a view of the village.

For as long as Daisy could remember, at the end of every summer, the villagers had taken all that they could carry up to the ruined castle and locked themselves in the dungeon. Here they spread rugs and blankets and a few reminders of home. Everyone settled in for many days of hiding. This meant quiet, no fires, and only cold porridge, beans and bacon scraps to eat. All because of the dragon.

It came every year on the first full moon of autumn. Hushed together in the dungeon, safe, if a little damp, the villagers would wait for the signs. A few would sense a tingle in the air, others would feel a hum in the castle walls. Then came a throbbing, whirring wind and a roar that made the villagers' hair stand on end. Not even the lookouts dared peep out as the monster, trailing purple smoke, came flying over the castle to land on the village green. Then, in the village it would stay, until the first frosts of winter.

And all that time there would be Daisy, huddled by the spyhole, eyes sharp for every move. She'd watched the dragon so often and so long, she felt she almost knew it. But no one else seemed to.

"There it goes again! Stomping around, knocking things down!" the villagers said, hearing bumps and clatters from the streets below.

"But there are no flames and it's only knocking over rubbish bins . . ." Daisy began, but no one would listen.

"Hush," said her mother. "Think how it might knock down one of us."

"It's been at the chimney pots again!" moaned the lookouts as they came off duty.

"But it was only one chimney, and it was an accident," Daisy tried to explain.

"Come away from there, Daisy, and hope it never gets you," said her father.

So Daisy joined the villagers, hunched in front of the cobwebby fireplace. There they talked of the harm the dragon could do and hatched plans to kill it. Daisy listened and said, "But it only tips over bins and a few chimney pots each year . . . " The villagers ignored her and said that they had to think about what such a huge beast *might* do.

Exactly. What *might* it do? thought Daisy, and she decided to find out once and for all.

Secretly, she wrapped up the last of her birthday cake and hid it in her nightgown. She stayed awake as the dungeon filled with snores. It became time for a change of lookouts. Daisy saw the fresh ones buckle on their boots and head out of the dungeon. She caught the heavy door before it closed. The lookouts were on their way and so was Daisy, shawl covering her nightgown and the cake. Tucked in the shadows behind the castle, Daisy ran unseen, taking the long track over the fields to reach the barn at the far side of the village.

The clip and scratch of monstrous claws echoed over rooftops and along the lanes. Keeping well away, Daisy sprinkled a trail of cake crumbs.
Some she spread through cottages,

some on the streets,

some over gardens,

and some into haystacks.

The last she scattered in a line to the barn.

There she climbed up, out of sight, but with a very good view of the village and, she hoped, perhaps a close one of the strange old dragon itself.

"Now, let's see what you *might* do," she whispered. And she smiled, for, just as she had thought, the dragon followed the cake-crumb trail, but not once did it poke its head in a house or step on a single cabbage patch or even hit a haystack. It took only the crumbs from the lanes and was soon on its way to the barn.

Now, she thought, I can tell everyone how the dragon cares for our village and will not harm us. High in the hay, Daisy ducked back as the monster lumbered near. Too late she caught the strong whiff of potato peelings, old porridge and worse. She was perched on top of the dragon's hay-covered store of smelly village rubbish.

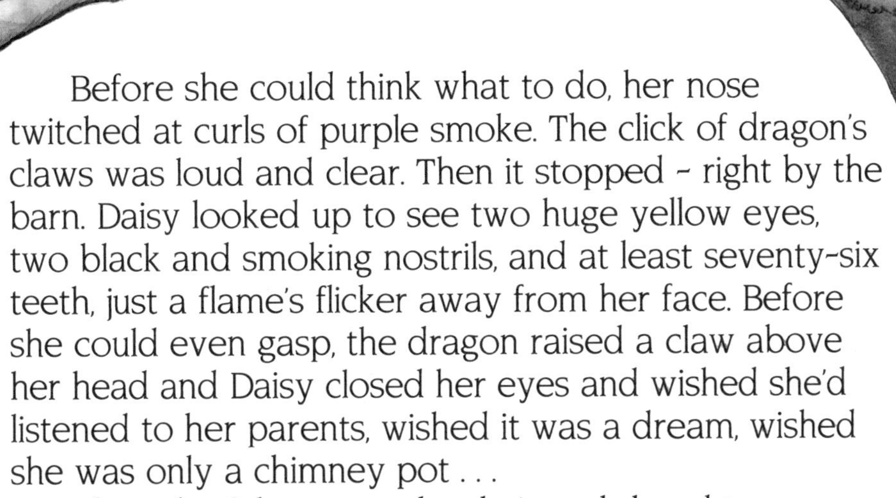

Before she could think what to do, her nose twitched at curls of purple smoke. The click of dragon's claws was loud and clear. Then it stopped – right by the barn. Daisy looked up to see two huge yellow eyes, two black and smoking nostrils, and at least seventy-six teeth, just a flame's flicker away from her face. Before she could even gasp, the dragon raised a claw above her head and Daisy closed her eyes and wished she'd listened to her parents, wished it was a dream, wished she was only a chimney pot . . .

Then she felt a tug at her hair and dared to open one eye. In front of her face was a tiny fish skin, skewered neatly on the end of a single dragon toenail. Then it was gone, slurped sharply in one blink of the dragon's moon-eyes. Daisy laughed and knew at once what the dragon might do next.

With a flick of its tail and a swish of its wings, the creature lifted Daisy on to its back. Then she was up, over the chimney pots, flying in the glow of the dawn and the purple haze of smoke. Daisy saw the lookouts shout as the dragon carried her to the castle. Soon the towers bristled with bows and arrows as the dragon flew close for the first time ever. Daisy knew she must be brave and leaned forward, past the creature's wings.

"It's me! Don't fire! It's me," she shouted.

Weapons were lowered and the villagers gasped as the dragon circled and landed in the courtyard with a gruff snort of smoke.

The villagers soon saw the gentle nature of the beast and realised they had nothing to fear. Daisy promised never to go off without a word again and in return the grown-ups promised to listen more to their children.

Every autumn the dragon was made a welcome guest at the barn (although the villagers first dug an extra well and brought in extra fire buckets, just in case). Litter was never a problem in the village, which became known for its excellent fertiliser. And every year the castle courtyard was specially decorated and people would come from far and wide to watch the dragon and, in later years, her babies too, light the candles on Daisy's cake.

The Bad-Tempered Bogle

by Jane Launchbury

Some people have fairies at the bottom of their gardens, but old Mrs Appleyard had something much nastier. She had a bogle at the bottom of her garden.

It arrived one dark winter night, when the wind was howling through the trees and rain was beating down in sheets. The bogle was in a bad mood. An exceptionally bad mood, even for a bogle. It had been flooded out of its cosy burrow by the river. Not only was it cold and wet, it was homeless too. It stamped its big flat feet in fury and gnashed its rotten yellow teeth. Staring wildly about with evil orange eyes, it saw just the thing it was looking for, at the bottom of Mrs Appleyard's garden.

Earlier that year, Mrs Appleyard had put up a nestbox for owls. There were no birds in it now, but there was a hibernating squirrel. The bogle had its own ideas about the best use for the box. It would be just right for its new home - too high to flood and, most importantly, it had a roof. With a great shriek it flung itself up the tree, thrashing its tail wildly.

The squirrel awoke with a start to see two big leathery ears, which sprouted great tufts of ginger hair, appear at the entrance hole. One look was enough. It didn't wait to see any more of whatever monstrous beast was attached to them. It hurled itself out of the box and ran off into the storm as fast as it could.

The bogle chuckled to itself and squeezed in through the entrance hole. The box wasn't quite as big as it had looked from the ground, and getting in was rather more difficult than it had anticipated. Still, it was dry and would do for the time being.

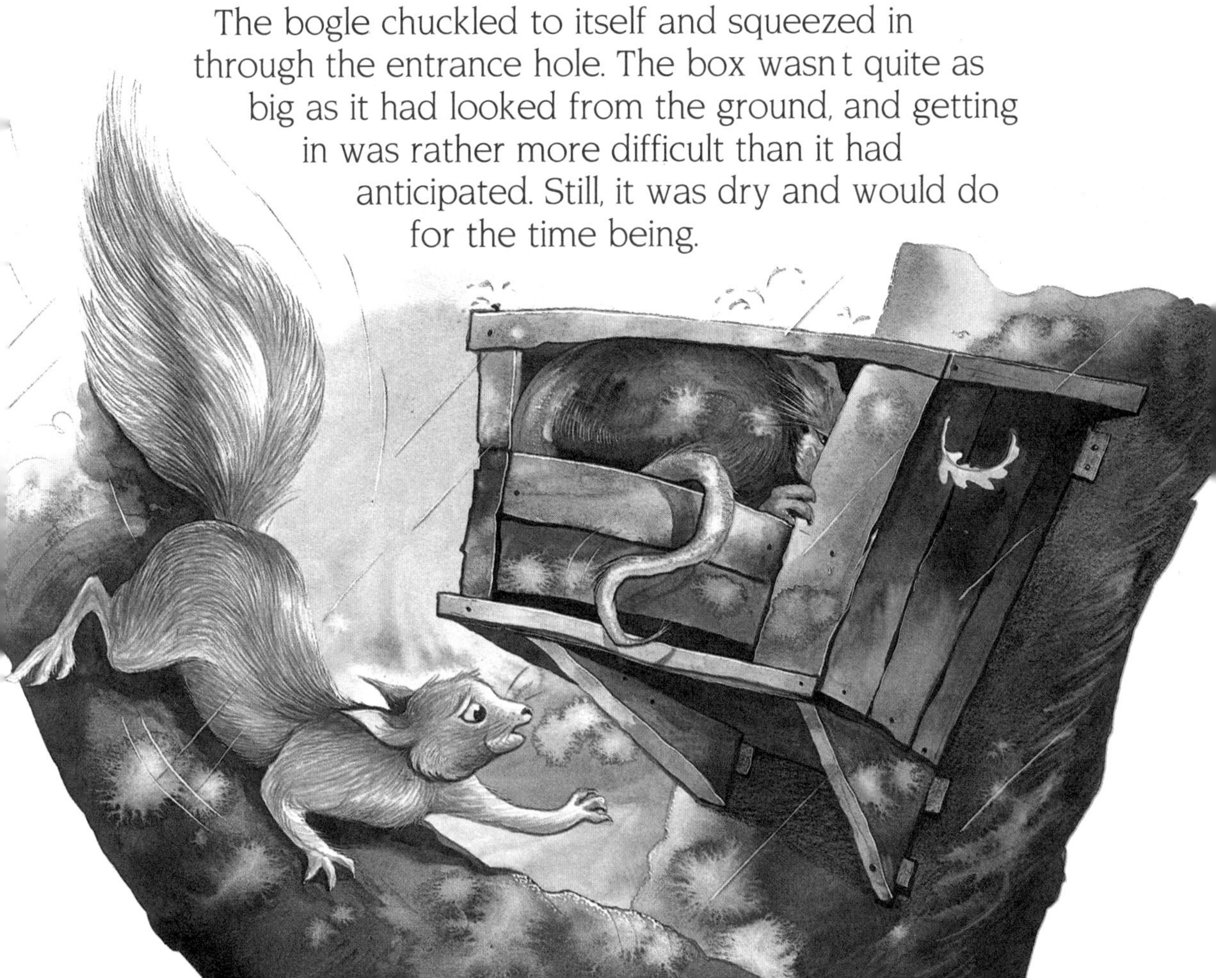

The next day the bogle decided that its new residence was distinctly lacking in creature comforts. It was too small, too draughty, it leaked, and it was full of creepy-crawlies. By sunset the bogle started to feel hungry, and by the time it ventured out, its stomach was rumbling in a disgusting manner. Rain was still pouring down when the bogle clambered out of the tree and stomped up through Mrs Appleyard's garden towards her little cottage. There was a pleasant orange glow coming from one of the windows. The bogle scrambled up a slippery drainpipe, landed with a plop on the windowsill and peered inside.

In the sitting-room of the cottage, Mrs Appleyard was sitting in a comfortable rocking-chair beside a blazing fire. She was drinking a steaming mug of tea and eating a boiled egg with Marmite soldiers. On the other side of the fireplace was a contented-looking dog, curled up on a pile of blankets.

Outside, the bogle's stomach rumbled so loudly that Mrs Appleyard thought the storm was getting worse and put some more logs on the fire.

"What a night," she said to her dog. "Thank goodness we're in our cosy cottage and not outside like all those poor wild creatures." Then she got up and gave the dog some of her Marmite soldiers and a saucer of tea.

The bogle sat on the windowsill and glowered in through the glass. Now that was what it called a proper home. It wouldn't be too difficult to achieve either. The bogle had one very unpleasant magical power. All it had to do to get people in its power was to make them cry . . . which was, of course, the very thing the nasty bogle had in mind. As soon as it could make Mrs Appleyard cry, it could start a new life, comfortable in that little cottage. It chuckled to itself, this would be easy! So it decided to start right away . . . it would scare the old lady into crying.

The bogle took a deep breath and let out a mournful wail. At the same time it clattered on the windowpane with its claws and its scaly tail. The noise was terrifying! But old Mrs Appleyard was rather hard of hearing and the dog had started barking, so she didn't hear the bogle at all.

"Quiet now, Jess," she said to the dog, "it's only the wind howling down the chimney." Then she got up and went over to the window to close the curtains. The bogle saw her coming and pulled its most ferocious face. It bared its big yellow teeth and pressed its horrible warty face against the glass.

But Mrs Appleyard had left her spectacles over by the fire and she didn't see the bogle at all.

The bogle was furious. It stamped its feet so hard that it skidded on the wet windowsill and fell off into a big puddle. Its stomach gave another rumble like thunder, and it remembered that it was still hungry. It stomped around the outside of the cottage until it saw a tiny window that wasn't properly shut. It scrambled up a creeper and fiddled with the window latch. The window swung open a few centimetres, and the bogle squeezed inside.

It was in the larder, and what a glorious sight! Mrs Appleyard had spent all day cooking big fruitcakes and filling jars with preserves. The bogle was delighted. It sat on the larder floor and had a feast. It stuffed itself silly. It poured damson jam and chutney over the fruitcakes, then wallowed around slurping up the delicious mess. It also found a flagon of elderflower wine and guzzled half of that.

When it had finished, it was so fat and dizzy that it could hardly squeeze back out of the window, let alone stagger down the garden. It chuckled contentedly, for it was certain that when Mrs Appleyard saw all her food gone the next morning, she would begin to cry.

The bogle burped and started to scramble up the tree to its nestbox. It was hard work. Then it shoved its head and shoulders through the entrance hole and started hauling itself in. It heaved and grunted, but it had eaten so much that it had grown too fat to get back into the box. So the bad-tempered bogle had to spend the rest of the night under a holly bush. It got very wet, covered in prickles, and it had an awful stomach-ache. Still, the next night it would be cosy inside the cottage, it was sure of that. Mrs Appleyard would soon be in floods of tears about her larder.

But the bogle was wrong. Mrs Appleyard was in a good mood when she got up for breakfast. She was somewhat surprised to find the mess in her larder but, when she saw the open window, she thought the squirrels and mice had been in.

"Those poor wild creatures must have been ever so hungry last night," she said. "I shall have to put out more scraps for them today."

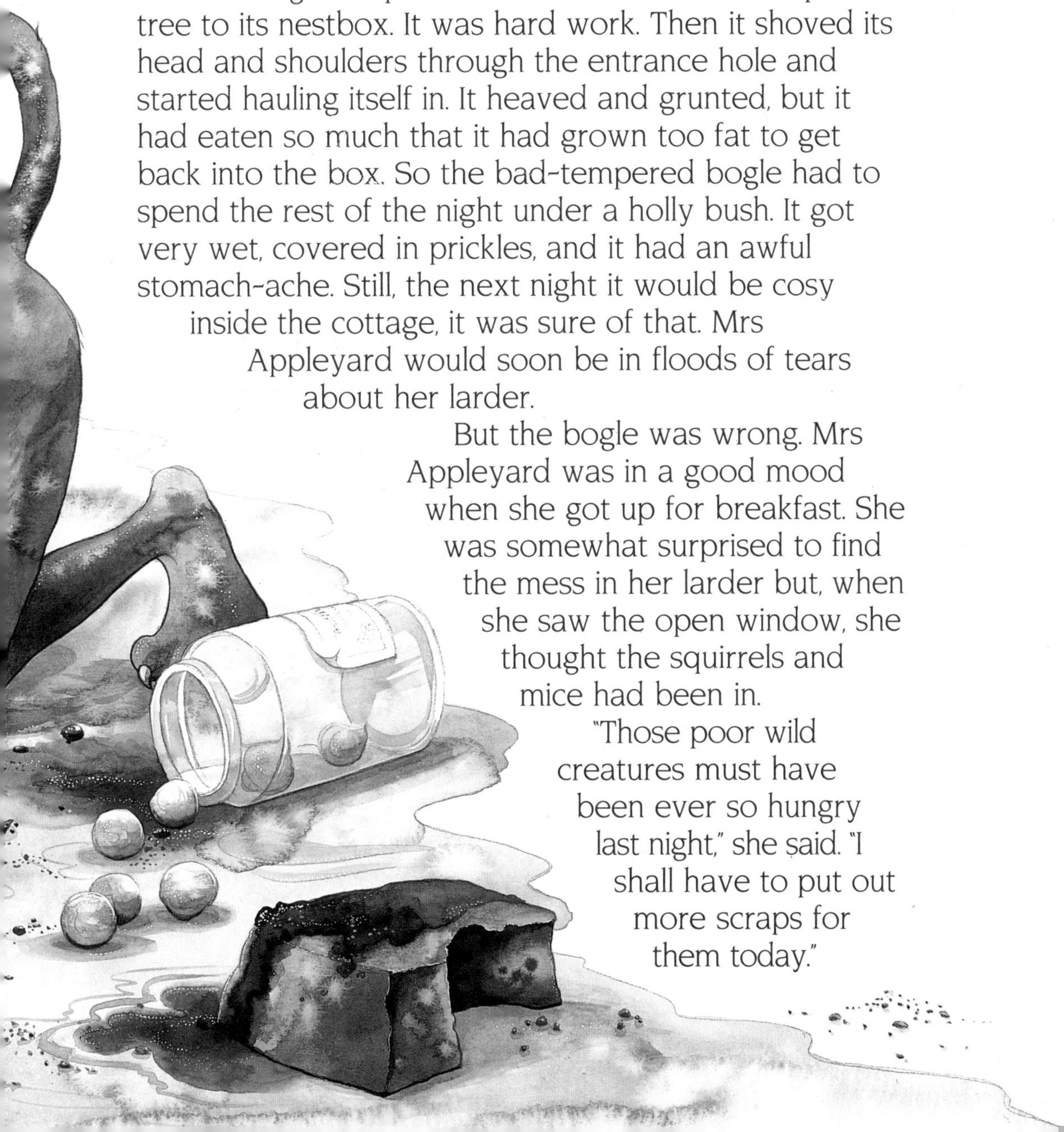

The bogle couldn't believe it. Mrs Appleyard was as cheerful as ever when she went outside to hang her washing on the line. She was even singing a happy song. The bogle gnashed its teeth and stamped its feet. No sooner had the old lady gone back inside than it climbed up on the washing-line and bit right through it. All the lovely clean washing fell down into the mud. But so did the bogle — it had got its big feet tangled up in a pair of baggy bloomers and it fell flat on its face in the muddiest place! It gnashed its teeth and then it thought that the old lady would surely cry when she saw her washing in the mud, and it cheered up a bit.

Mrs Appleyard wasn't pleased when she saw what had happened to her washing, but she didn't cry. In fact she smiled and said, "It serves me right, really, I should have replaced that old washing-line months ago." Then she went back indoors, rinsed the mud off the washing and put it in front of the fire to dry.

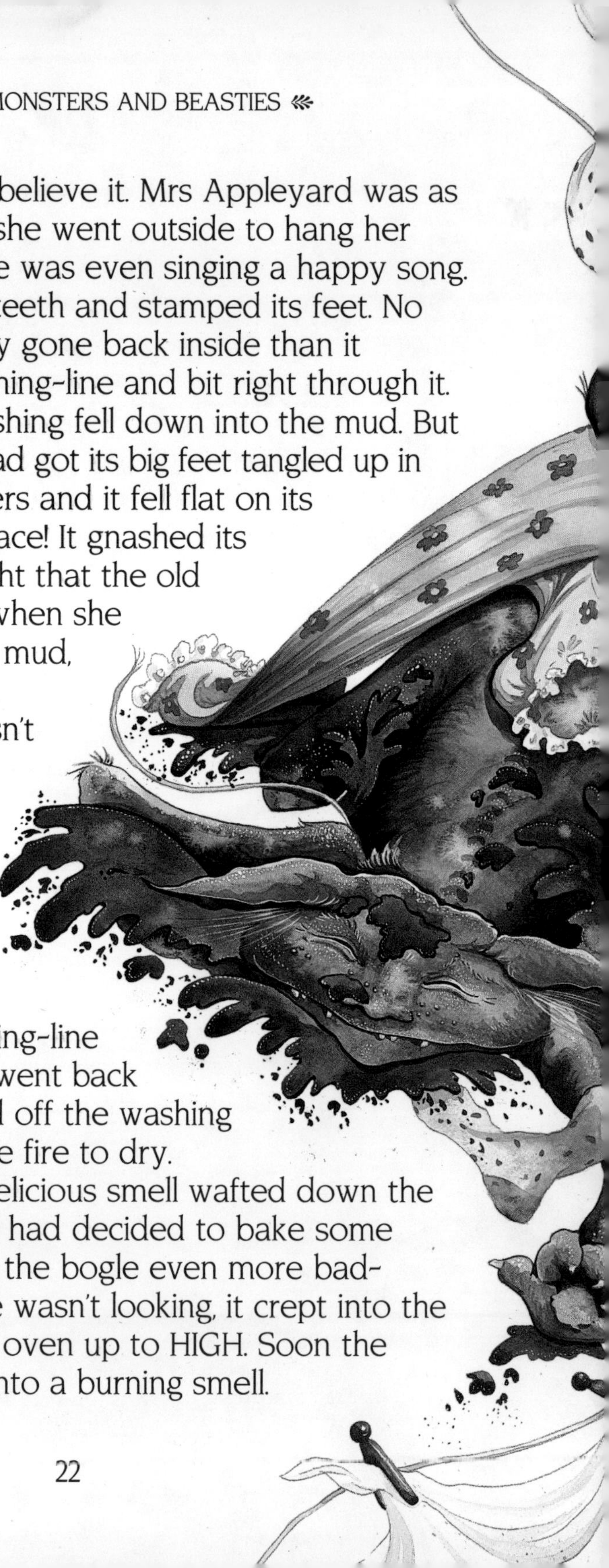

That afternoon a delicious smell wafted down the garden. Mrs Appleyard had decided to bake some more cakes. This made the bogle even more bad-tempered. So when she wasn't looking, it crept into the kitchen and turned the oven up to HIGH. Soon the delicious smell turned into a burning smell.

That should upset her enough, thought the bogle.

"You silly old lady," said Mrs Appleyard to herself. "Burning all those lovely cakes. But never mind, I'll put them out for the wild birds and animals, they won't mind."

The bogle certainly did mind, though. It didn't want burnt cakes for dinner, it had been expecting tea and cream cakes in the cottage by now, waited on by an obedient servant. This was too much, it couldn't bear sitting outside in the cold and dark, looking in through a lighted window at what it couldn't have. So it climbed up on to the roof and disconnected the electricity supply. At least that way it wouldn't be able to see what it was missing, and life would be very unpleasant in the dark for the old lady. So unpleasant, it thought hopefully, that she would cry about it.

But Mrs Appleyard didn't cry. She fumbled about a bit, and soon had a candle lit. Then she lit a couple of old oil lamps and put a few more logs on the fire. "Just like old times," she said happily to the dog. "I never did like electric lights as much." Then she settled back in her chair, rocking gently until she fell asleep.

The bogle sat on the window-sill and peered furiously into the cottage. The candles and oil lamps made it look even cosier than ever. Then it got into a real rage; it had run out of evil ideas.

On top of that, another storm had started and it would have to spend the night in that poky old box full of creepy-crawlies. The bogle huddled against the windowpane for warmth, feeling very sorry for itself.

Then something happened which had never happened before. The bogle started feeling sorry for Mrs Appleyard. For all those beastly things it had done to try and make her cry. It shivered as rain plopped on to its head. Then it felt something warm running down its nose. It wasn't rain at all . . . it was a tear. The bogle itself was crying. It had never cried before, but now it felt so miserable that it couldn't help it.

As it cried, strange things began happening. Matted ginger and brown fur sprouted all over its body, but the bogle was too fed up to notice. A tear dropped off the end of one of its whiskers. This puzzled it, as it didn't remember ever having had whiskers! Its legs lost their scaly, leathery skin and became all furry.

Another tear plopped to the ground, and the bogle felt even stranger. It didn't feel like a bogle any more. In fact it had forgotten what it felt like to be a bogle.

Just then the cottage door opened and Mrs Appleyard came out with a bowl of dog food for the hedgehogs. As she bent to put it down she noticed something furry cowering under the window. It looked like a very bedraggled cat.

"Oh, you poor little thing," she said, scooping it up into her arms. "I've never seen such a sad, wet pussycat in all my life. You must come inside and dry out in front of the fire." She carried the bewildered cat into the cottage and put it down beside Jess. The scruffy tabby nestled close to the friendly dog, enjoying the warmth of the fire. Then Mrs Appleyard gave them both a big dish of cream, and as much food as they could eat.

The wind howled around the cottage that night and the rain lashed against the windowpanes, but old Mrs Appleyard and her pets were warm and dry inside. And, at the bottom of the garden, the squirrel climbed back into the nestbox, to sleep in peace for the rest of the winter.

Monsters You May Have Met

by Maria Gordon

Not so long ago, just as the sun was rising, three ugly monsters were eating breakfast. They all had excellent monster manners, which meant that they were totally disgusting. They shoved each other out of the way, walked all over their food and dribbled on it.

They were busy making a terrible mess when they heard a loud creak from somewhere nearby. The monsters froze and listened, but they heard no more. So they carried on slobbering over mouldy fruit and dead monster legs.

There were a few more creaks, but the monsters were too busy feasting and paid no attention. But then came a particularly loud groaning sound followed by a dreadful thump.

This the monsters could not ignore.

"Oooh! Pickle me pinchers! It's a giant one coming to get us. Run, everyone, run!" shouted the first. He turned, scurried across the flat, empty space, and into a dark cave.

"Glub, slop, blug!" said the second, hastily spitting out a mouthful of toenails. He, too, was soon in the cave, legs whirling and slashing.

"Help, Mummy!" squeaked the third, scuttling as fast as he could and catching up only just in time.

The monsters watched as the giant one pounded across the bare ground in front of the cave. The floor shook, and the monsters shook too. They held their breath, waiting for the trembling to fade as the giant one crashed off into the distance. For now, the monsters were safe. To them the cave was vast, but it would be a tight squeeze for the giant one, even lying down. The monsters sighed with relief in the darkness.

"B-b-by all the hairs on me legs, I never seen such a b-b-bunch. D-d-don't tell me you's all scared of a little pounding and shaking?" said a strange voice.

The three monsters jumped in surprise and collided in a heap.

"P-p-pardon me, my little garbage eaters. But why don't you finish b-b-breakfast?" It was a fourth monster who'd spoken. He sat, bug-eyed and beefy, on a ledge above them.

The first monster stared up at him and spoke:

"There's a giant one out there. Fry me feelers, but we ain't goin' out while he's about."

The bug-eyed monster laughed at this. Then he leaped from his ledge and swung down on a rope. His legs skimmed the heads of the other three.

"B-b-by all the spots on me chest, I never seen a giant one that could get me," he boasted.

"Just shows you's got all yer brains in yer legs," said the first monster.

"Yes, and I wish yer'd keep yer smelly legs out of me ears," said the second.

"Help, Mummy!" said the third.

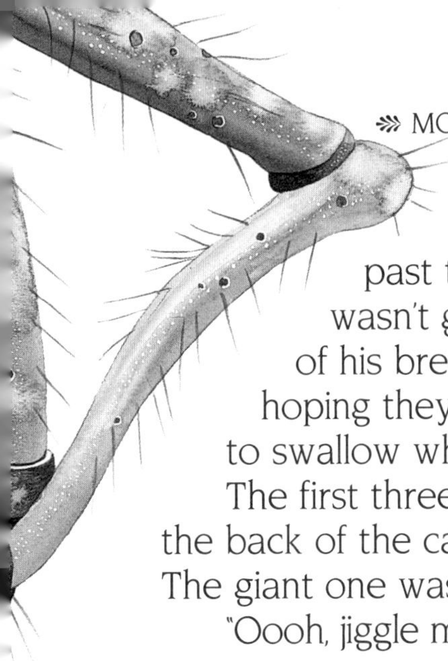

Bug-eye laughed again and pushed past the others to the cave entrance. He wasn't going to let a giant one get in the way of his breakfast. He'd set his traps and was hoping they'd caught something nice and wriggly to swallow whole.

The first three monsters settled into the darkness at the back of the cave. Then the pounding began again. The giant one was returning.

"Oooh, jiggle me joints! It's back!" whispered the first monster.

"Gulp!" went the second.

"Help, Mummy!" squealed the third and they all flattened themselves against the cave walls. But Bug-eye didn't move. His eyes were fixed on something across the bare land outside the cave.

"B-b-by all the glue in me traps, I's caught something big and juicy. Yum. B-b-breakfast, here I come!" and the greedy thing was off before the others could even burp. The three monsters looked on as Bug-eye scuttled out. They saw the giant one stop. They heard it cackle. They saw its shadow creep over the greedy monster and saw him stop too late . . . In one short splat it was over. And so was Bug-eye, squashed by the giant one.

"Help, Mummy!" cried all three monsters huddled in the blackness. But the giant one was done. It was soon far away from the cave and never even poked its head in the entrance. The three monsters were safe for now. They would live to tell the tale of the foolish, greedy Bug-eye to their many grandchildren. But it was a very long time before they set out for their supper . . .

To the giant one, though, it was just another ordinary day. All she had done was to get out of bed, walk out of her bedroom and then return . . . just in time to spot a quite horrible-looking spider crossing her bedroom floor. But ever since the time Miss Muffet ate breakfast outdoors she never had liked creepy-crawlies — especially spiders.

How about you? Are there beasties under your bed too?

Prince Timo and the Rainbow Birds

by Maria Gordon

The newlywed prince and princess set sail on a cloudless summer morning; the royal bird hunt had begun. The prince was proud to have his bride on board. He watched her sharpening arrows with the sailors and his father, the king. Prince Timo knew Corrina's eyes would light up at the huge flocks of birds across the ocean. She was one of the finest archers in the land.

"Full speed!" Timo urged the captain. He was sure the decks would soon be piled higher than ever before with the wonderful, dazzling feathers.

As the sun rose on the third day, the whole crew cheered. The lookout had spied a flock of birds wheeling in the east. By noon, the hum of whirring wings filled the air and the shooting began. The sailors gasped at Timo and Corrina's aim and speed. Arrows filled the sky till darkness fell. A roasted bird feast was served. Everyone felt this would indeed be a special hunt.

The storm hit without warning.

"Stay below!" yelled the prince to Corrina. He climbed up to the main deck. There he joined his father and the crew, who were struggling to keep the ship afloat. Salt spray lashed his face and the ropes cut into his hands. Then the wind slammed against him, pushing him up to the rails and over, into the black and pitching sea. A cry went up, but he was gone, lost to the storm.

For days the ship circled, searching for the prince. Corrina could not eat or rest. There was no sign of Timo.

Eventually water and food ran low and only then did the princess allow the crew to take herself and the king back to land.

Many miles away, the rainbow birds were still circling. Beneath them lay several tiny islands, all the same. But on one, the waves had washed up something grey and lifeless. Then a crab took a pinch and the crooked bundle stirred. It was the prince. His throat hurt, his lips stung, he was sore all over, but he was alive. He gazed at the islands, then out at the ocean. His heart fell. Was the ship sunk? Where was Corrina? His father? The crew?

With tears in his eyes, Timo looked up at the birds overhead. Only then did he notice their nests. No one had ever found the land of the rainbow birds. He was the first to watch them fly to and from the big driftwood dishes set in the strange island trees. And even in his sadness, the prince had to laugh at the bright, fluffy chicks leaning and squawking over the edges. His laughter caught in his parched throat.

Right by him, one bird swooped down and dipped its beak in a tiny silvery pool in the curled tip of a branch. The bird flew back and dropped the liquid into the beak of its chick. Timo stepped up to the branch and took a taste from one of the little pools. It was water, dew collected in the cool of the night.

Thank you, he thought and went from branch to branch, sipping the water until his throat was eased. He knew he could fish for food, but first it was time to explore. He soon saw that a clump of the black trees grew on each island. All had branches but no leaves. The trees sprouted not from soil, but a kind of grey, rubbery land.

On either side of each clump, Timo could see a curved bush with black floppy leaves. On every island the land stretched down to two black pits. Every few minutes wisps of steam rose from the pits and the land shook gently.

Volcanoes? Earthquakes? wondered the prince. He decided to try to escape from the islands as quickly as possible. First, he set about building a bonfire as a signal to passing ships. He gathered wood fallen from the nests. Rubbing two sticks together, he lit the woodpile. But, as he did so, the rainbow birds flew at him. They knocked Timo over and beat the fire out with their wings. Stunned, the prince watched them return to their nests. Then a touch of glowing ash fell to the ground. The whole island shuddered and the birds whistled in alarm.

Scared, Timo tried raft-building instead. He tugged on a young tree, trying to snap it at its base. But once again the birds flew at him and the ground trembled. Why did the rainbow birds ruin his work? He swam to the next island, but they stopped him there, too.

Timo was stumped. He realised he could only wait for the sea to bring logs for a raft or ships to pass. Days went by. The prince swam, fished and waited. One morning he spotted the young rainbow birds beginning to fly. By evening, every bird on the island was in the air. Timo gasped. None were roosting. Instead, they flew wildly around his head, driving him into the sea. And there they kept him, bewildered, far, far from the island. Did they know him to be their hunter and wish he would drown? Timo thought this might be fair after the thousands of birds he had killed. But his thoughts were broken by a terrible roar.

A great wave pushed out from the islands. Then Timo saw the islands raising themselves up and heaving through the ocean, their craters lifted into the air. They crashed back on to the sea-foam and that was when Timo saw their eyes open. The islands were creatures! Their leafy bushes were eyelids, the trees were hairs and the pits were blowholes. And he had set fires on their skins and pulled at their hairs. The birds were partners with the island beasts. They knew the massive creatures would dive when the young birds flew. The rainbow birds had protected their monster lands and they had saved him — their destroyer. But without the huge island-monsters how would he survive? He could only swim, hoping to find land or another great beast. He was amazed to see that the birds stayed with him.

And so were Corrina and her crew. Searching with a fresh ship, the princess had set course for the flock, puzzled by its slowness. A great shout went up as they discovered the prince in the waves beneath the rainbow birds.

From that day on the birds were never hunted. Royal ships watched over the island-monsters and any feathers found were valued more than ever. The prince and princess helped the king rule wisely. And, for the rest of their days, they continued to travel far, learning and teaching about the special lives of all the animals in their kingdom.

Once a Monster, Always a Monster

by Maria Gordon

Snodvig woke up with that cosy, full feeling that comes from eating people and falling asleep up an old sewer pipe. He smiled and licked his lips as he remembered yesterday's chase. It was always such fun when he'd made a meal of a sleeping guard or two and couldn't hold back the burps. This would always bring out the humans. But he liked the chase, picking bits of uniform out of his teeth and giggling as he looked back at the puny little creatures who could never outrun him. Then he'd find somewhere smelly, snug and hidden to sleep off the hunt and plan the next.

He had to be careful to visit places before the news of his dreadful deeds travelled ahead of him. It wasn't the same if the humans had a chance. So off he lumbered on his horrible, hairy legs, following the scent of people to a city far away.

Many passing mountain goat snacks later, Snodvig's path was crossed by a line of strange poles. These hummed and glowed around his knees as he lumbered near them. This made him cross so he ate these, too, enjoying the way they fizzed on his tongue. Then, clambering over a ridge, he drooled in surprise. What looked like a feast of humans was laid out in the valley below.

Our stinky beast could not know his people-scent trail had led to their city parade. Every year, they'd wheel out their inventions, from shine-in-the-dark-slippers to spray-on hats. Machines filled their every need, baking bread, picking fruit, even cleaning between their toes. There was no need to work now, only play.

The parade was made in luxurious steam cars along roads round the city, steam sweepers clearing the way.

"So fortunate are we, to have solved all our problems," they said. "And nothing can disturb our wonderful life because our Beast-Away Fence will hypnotise anything wild and dangerous, making it calm and tame." This, of course, was the very same fence that had fizzed so pleasantly on Snodvig's tongue.

Snodvig sniffed the air, his eyes scouring the delicious-looking line of people just a few claw-lengths away. They banged and clanked a good deal, but none had weapons and they all seemed nicely plump and ripe. It didn't take our monster long to decide on a good scare and shake-up instead of his usual nightly raid. He picked up his paws, crashed out of the trees, and roared at the people at the end of the parade.

"Goodness," they laughed. "This creature has been so tamed by the Beast-Away Fence that it's shouting with joy and wants to join the parade."

Then Snodvig was caught by a huge metal arm that zipped out from the back of the very last parade car. Its cold metal pincers grabbed the monster round his middle, lifting him off the ground, roarless and frozen in mid-slash, his eyes wide with astonishment. Up and up they raised him, like a giant, hairy balloon behind all the cars. By now, everyone had turned to watch and the crowd cheered.

All might have been well if the inventors had kept our beastie up in the air. As it was, they drove Snodvig into the city and set him down at their outdoor feast. Now, guns and cannonballs were nothing to Snodvig. He'd snapped a thousand swords and used arrows as toothpicks. But humans without fear he'd never met before.

Snodvig was in shock. He sat motionless while the children tickled his toes and the grown-ups fed him veggie-burgers. After cream puffs and treacle tart, the people bundled him with them on to the moving pavement as they all set off for an evening's song and dance. Merry voices filled the city square and the steam organ started up. In fact, it blasted right into Snodvig's ear. He blinked and realised that he hadn't done anything nasty for a whole afternoon. He'd managed not to eat a single, juicy human. He'd let them stroke his matted hair and pat his paws. And here he was, joining in their joyful celebrations. This was . . . absolutely terrible!

With the most humungous roar you ever heard, Snodvig smashed the organ, pulled up the moving pavement, scooped up six screaming inventors and ran off with them into the night, followed only by a squeaking mechanical waiter trying to serve them home-made lemonade.

Which just goes to show that it's never wise to think every problem's solved. There'll always be bigger and better ones round the corner or over the fence. Also - don't forget - never take a monster home to dinner unless you've tamed him yourself.

The Mauve Monster

by Jane Launchbury

Caroline stood on tiptoe, on top of two telephone directories, and stretched and stretched until she was another centimetre taller. She peeped out of the tiny circle of glass that was just above her nose and gave a gasp of delight. The world outside had gone mauve! The sky was glowing and everything in the street shimmered in strange shades of mauve and violet. There had been a heavy frost in the night and tiny ice crystals sparkled everywhere in the winter sunshine. The ordinary, grey world outside looked magical. Much more interesting than it had ever looked through the yellow or green pieces of the stained glass panel that was set into the front door.

She watched the mauve milkman come up the garden path, with two bottles of mauve milk. Then the mauve man next door started up his car and clouds of shimmering mauve gas came from the exhaust pipe. Several pale purple people passed and then the postman appeared at the gate, and right behind him, reading a postcard over his shoulder, was something *very* strange indeed.

It had four long, spindly legs and a long neck, and was not unlike an enormous giraffe. Only this creature was mauve, with large violet eyes, and a shaggy mane and tail like a wild horse. Caroline gasped and slipped off the telephone directories. The post came through the letterbox and she pressed her face to the glass again. There, through the green glass section that she looked through every morning, was the postman, with his familiar green face. But there was no sign of the strange monster. She stretched up until she could see out of the mauve glass again, and held her breath.

There it was again, following the postman across the street to Mrs Hopkins' house.

Then it stopped in the middle of the road just as the school bus appeared, heading straight for it.

"Oh no!" whispered Caroline, shutting her eyes. When she opened them again, her right eye was beside a yellow glass segment and all she could see was the school bus, and no sign of the monster. Her mum rushed up to open the door, scolding her daughter for being so slow, But Caroline had just enough time to stretch up and catch a glimpse, through the mauve glass, of long spindly legs and a happy, mauve face peeping round the edge of the bus.

No one on the bus had seen anything strange and they all thought Caroline had gone loopy. All that day at school Caroline thought about the monster and couldn't wait to get back home to have another look for it. As luck would have it, they were all sent home early because of a bad weather forecast. A strong storm was coming and the winds were already blowing harder than normal.

Caroline jumped off the school bus and ran up the garden path with her door key in her hand. She flung the door open, jumped over the doormat, and then something dreadful happened.

The strong wind caught the door and slammed it shut with such a crash that the stained glass panel fell right out and smashed into pieces on the ground. Caroline's mum was furious. Partly she was cross with Caroline for being careless, but most of all she was cross because she knew that they couldn't afford to replace the lovely stained glass.

Mum fitted a piece of wood into the hole where the glass had been, while Caroline swept up the broken glass. She did it slowly and carefully so that she wouldn't cut herself on the hundreds of tiny shards. As she filled the dustpan for the third time she saw that there was one small unbroken piece – it was the mauve glass she'd been looking through that morning. She put it in her pocket, and as soon as she'd finished, she took it to her room.

She stood at the window and peered at the back garden through the piece of glass. Everything was mauve again, but without the sunshine it didn't sparkle, and there was not a sign of the monster.

That night there was a terrible storm. The wind howled around the house, knocking tiles off the roof and breaking branches from the trees. In the middle of the night there was an extra strong gust and a horrible tearing, screaming noise.

Caroline slept through the whole storm and woke when sunshine streamed into her room. She opened the curtains to see that the old apple tree in the garden had fallen on to the lawn and the garden looked as though it had been a battlefield. Wondering whether mauve glass would make things look any better, she held it to her eye.

There it was again! The mauve monster was strolling around in her garden.

Bold as brass, it sauntered over to the uprooted tree and pawed at the loose earth. Then it looked straight at Caroline, winked, and peered very closely at the ground where the tree used to grow, nuzzling it gently. It seemed to be trying to tell her something.

Caroline put down the mauve glass and stared out of the bedroom window. There was definitely no monster visible. She peered through the glass again but the monster had vanished.

She ran down the stairs and out into the garden in her dressing-gown and slippers and went straight to the old apple tree. In the loose soil where the roots had been pulled out of the ground something was glistening. It was a gold coin! She rolled up her sleeves and scrabbled about until she found seven more coins, then she ran inside to tell her mum the good news.

Some time later, they received the money from the sale of the gold coins, and not only was it enough for Caroline and her mum to have a lovely holiday, but there was also plenty left to have a new stained glass window put in the front door. At Caroline's special request, the old piece of mauve glass was included in the design, and this time it was positioned exactly in line with her eyes so she could see through it without stretching.

Although she looked through the glass every day while she waited for the school bus, she never did see the mauve monster again, and before long she had grown so tall that she had to bend down to look through the mauve circle. This was almost as uncomfortable as it had been standing on tiptoe on the telephone directories, so she grew out of the habit. The mauve monster does still visit, but Caroline's baby brother is not quite tall enough to see through the mauve glass . . . yet.

The Weather-Dragon

by Jane Launchbury

S E W N

A strong gust of wind caught the wings of the weather-dragon. Metal creaked and groaned as it turned on the old spindle, pointing the dragon's head towards cold, grey mountains. Henry glanced up at the weather vane, shivered and pulled the hood of his cloak over his head. It kept the cold wind out of his ears and fell forward over his eyes, obscuring the view of the wizard's sinister castle.

Perched on its metal spike at the top of the wizard's tower, the weather-dragon looked down on the castle, the village and the surrounding fields. Its metal body and wings were blackened by smoke and soot from the wizard's chimneys. It had been perched there for years, turning relentlessly.

The wind grew stronger, swirling leaves and twigs wildly around the children working in the wizard's fields.

Rain drove into the folds of their cloaks and stung their hands and faces. Most stopped working and ran to their homes, but Henry carried on. The wizard would be watching, and he was already in trouble for disobedience. If he didn't continue until sunset he'd face one of the wizard's horrible punishments.

Heavy clouds raced across the sky and the silhouette of the castle grew darker. Then came a mighty flash of lightning and the crashing, rumbling roar of thunder. Henry threw himself to the ground, hiding under his heavy cloak. But a huge gust of wind lifted it up like a sail, spiralling him into the air. He grabbed a tree, pulling himself to safety, then watched as a vortex of dust and debris swirled upwards. It raced along the castle walls and rose, up and up until it hit the weather-dragon and sent it into a frenzied spin. Henry stared as the metal creature was lifted off its spindle, its whirling body and wings making a terrific whistling.

Lightning blinded him momentarily, and after the thunder there was a strange stillness. Henry looked up, but the whirlwind had vanished and so had the weather-dragon. He ran towards the village path, but stopped in his tracks. There, at the edge of the field, was the battered shape of the weather-dragon.

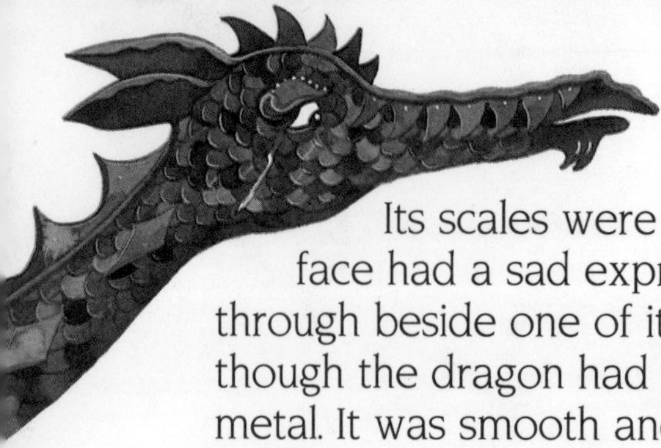

Its scales were beautifully tooled and its long face had a sad expression. A streak of gold shone through beside one of its eyes and it really looked as though the dragon had been crying. Henry touched the metal. It was smooth and silky. He stroked it softly, then tucked it under his arm and set off toward the village.

Soon he was at the door of his friend, Will Wayland. Henry carried the weather-dragon into Will's workshop and set it down on one of the benches. A blazing fire roared in the corner, for Will was the village blacksmith. The big man examined the dragon. Its tail, neck and wings were badly bent.

"This is beautiful, but it's the wizard's weather vane, isn't it, Henry?" said Will. Henry nodded and noticed that a look of fear crept into his friend's eyes. "Anything could happen if I try to bend this back into shape in my fire," said Will sadly.

"Please try," begged Henry. "It looks so sad and I think it wants our help." The blacksmith sighed and smiled at the child. Then he thought of the wizard. What might happen if he was found with the weather-dragon in his workshop? He would have to give a good reason, which could only be that he was repairing it.

Henry worked the bellows as Will lifted the dragon into the flames and began to straighten the bent metal as it grew soft and glowed in the heat. The fire roared and flames curled round the dragon's body as the strong man worked. Suddenly, the tools were wrenched from his hands and sparks showered from the fire. Will jumped back and dragged Henry with him.

Man and boy watched in amazement as the dragon started to breathe and move in the flames. It lifted itself up and turned its sad face towards Will and Henry. Then it smiled so beautifully that they knew it meant them no harm. Will opened the big double doors and the dragon rose gracefully and flew out into the dark, stormy night.

Henry and Will rushed outside, watching as the glowing dragon flew straight up to the wizard's castle. As it moved away, the fiery dragon grew larger and larger until it looked huge, perched on top of the tower which had been its home for so long. Then, with no warning, it roared and sent a great river of flames cascading on to the castle below, setting fire to all the wizard's laboratories. Loud explosions rent the air and sparks of all colours swirled out of the inferno, up into the clouds. Still the dragon scorched the castle with its fiery breath as the sky above glowed red.

The villagers assembled on the green, watching in silence at first, uncertain what was happening. Then they realised that the creature on the tower was destroying their enemy, the wizard, who had ruled and bullied them for so long.

They cheered as the tower fell and the dragon flew into the sky. Although the wind was still blowing strongly, the fire had remained completely contained within the castle walls. No stray sparks had blown on to the thatched roofs in the village and all was safe.

As the dragon flew back to the village, its fiery glow faded and it shrank to its previous size. Above the thunder's rumble, Henry heard a metallic clatter as the weather-dragon fell into Will's yard. It was restored to its original shape but now shone gold as though its metal had been freshly polished. Henry touched it gingerly - it was still warm.

"Thank you, thank you, weather-dragon," he said, kissing its cheek. There was a green flash, and there, instead of the dragon, stood a beautiful young princess. Her smile was exactly like the dragon's, and she cried tears of joy as she hugged Henry.

The villagers celebrated as they heard the princess's story. The wizard had taken over her home and driven her family out. He had kept her as a servant, but she had refused to work, and in fury he had cast a spell, turning her into the weather-dragon. Release from the dragon's shape was only possible with the kiss of a young man.

Over the next year, the princess traced her lost family, and the castle was rebuilt from the ashes. She and Henry became inseparable and as soon as they were old enough, they married. Will Wayland created a beautiful golden weathercock for them, and to this day it can be seen turning in the breeze above the castle.